P9-DIY-082

Ashley Bryan's ABC

of

African American

·POETRY·

For my sister, ERNESTINE
And to the memory of her husband,
KENNETH HASKINS
Great Educator, Great Friend

Ashley Bryan's ABC

of African American

• POETRY •

Aladdin Paperbacks

New York   London   Toronto   Sydney   Singapore

First Aladdin Paperbacks edition January 2001

Illustrations copyright © 1997 by Ashley Bryan

Aladdin Paperbacks
An imprint of Simon & Schuster
Children's Publishing Division
1230 Avenue of the Americas
New York, NY 10020

All rights reserved, including the right of reproduction in whole or in part in any form.

Also available in an Atheneum Books for Young Readers hardcover edition

Designed by Ann Bobco/Nina Barnett

The text for this book was set in 12-point Journal.
The illustrations were done in tempera and gouache paintings.

Printed in Hong Kong
10 9 8 7 6 5 4 3 2 1

The Library of Congress has cataloged the hardcover edition as follows:

Bryan, Ashley.
Ashley Bryan's ABC of African American Poetry / Ashley Bryan.—1st ed.
p.   cm.
"A Jean Karl book."
Summary: A poem for each letter of the alphabet describes an aspect of the black experience.
ISBN: 0-689-81209-4 (hc.)
1. English language—Alphabet—Juvenile poetry. 2. Afro-Americans—Juvenile poetry.
3. Children's poetry, American. [1. Afro-Americans—Poetry. 2. American poetry—Afro-American
authors. 3. Alphabet.] I. Title.
PS3552.R848A69   1997   811'.54—dc20   [E] 96-25148
ISBN: 0-689-84045-4 (Aladdin pbk.)

Page 32 constitutes an extension of this copyright page.

·FOREWORD·

My ABC of African American poetry suggests a new way of working with the alphabet, not so much to teach the alphabet to the very young, but to introduce a world of poetry and art to all children. Generally alphabet books hold the first letter of whatever is presented. To do this alphabet book based on the first letter of the names of poets or from the first letter of the beginning word of a poem proved impossible.

There was also the problem of the length of poems. How could I have room enough for the illustration of a poem consisting of many stanzas or pages?

Then an idea opened this project to me. I'd use only the lines of each poem that inspired the image, and I'd capitalize the alphabet letter wherever it occurred in those lines.

I worked from a list of over seventy African American poets, drawn from my books at hand. I decided to include one African American spiritual, the root of Black song and poetry.

As I read, images sprang from the lines of the poets. I began sketching from the work of many more poets than one book would allow. Finally, I chose the sketches that offered a balanced play of images and did finished paintings from them in tempera paints and gouache colors.

You may find African American poets you know in this collection and others you might like to get to know. The acknowledgments list sources for all of the poems. Some poems are complete, others are fragments. I hope you will seek out the whole poems and go on to discover more work of these African American artists.

Ashley Bryan

And God stepped out on space,
And he looked around and said:
I'm lonely —
I'll make me a world.

JAMES WELDON JOHNSON

B

Black girl black girl
lips as curved as cherries
full as grape bunches
sweet as blackberries

DUDLEY RANDALL

C

(SOJOURNER TRUTH)

Comes walking barefoot
out of slavery

ancestress
childless mother

following the stars
her mind a star

ROBERT HAYDEN

D

Dear Noah: Please save me a spot
Exposed to the sun, where the Mice are *not*;
But if I *must* share my chamber, the Ant
Is the one I should welcome. Yours: L. E. Phant

COUNTEE CULLEN

Each man
a string on the harp
doing its own destiny
no one pushing
no one behind
each man
the end
and the beginning
of harmony

E HENRY DUMAS

There are words like **F**reedom
Sweet and wonderful to say.
On my heart-strings freedom sings
All day everyday.

LANGSTON HUGHES

God never planted a garden
But He placed a keeper there;
And the keeper ever razed the ground
And built a city where
God cannot walk at the eve of day,
Nor take the morning air.

ANNE SPENCER

Harriet Tubman didn't take no stuff
Wasn't scared of nothing neither
Didn't come in this world to be no slave
And wasn't going to stay one either

ELOISE GREENFIELD

If I could imagine the shaping of Fate,
I would think of blackmen
Handling the sun.

RAYMOND PATTERSON

July. The conspiracy of colors —
Ketchup, marshmallows, the tub of ice,
Bacon strips floating in pale soup.
The sun, like a dragon spreading its tail,
Burns the blue air to ribbons.

RITA DOVE

I am **K**ojo. In West Afrika Kojo
means Unconquerable. My parents
named me the seventh day from my birth
in Black spirit, Black faith, Black communion.
I am Kojo. I am A Black.
And I Capitalize my name.

Do not call me out of my name.

GWENDOLYN BROOKS

the **L**eaves believe
such letting go is love
such love is faith
such faith is grace
such grace is god
i agree with the leaves

LUCILLE CLIFTON

My grandmothers were strong.
They followed plows and bent to toil.
They moved through fields sowing seed.
They touched earth and grain grew.
They were full of sturdiness and singing.
My grandmothers were strong.

MARGARET WALKER

Nothing happens only once,
Nothing happens only here,
Every love that lies asleep
Wakes today another year.

OWEN DODSON

The **O**ld of our people
are the elders of the race
and must be listened to,
must be looked after,
must be given meaningful work,
must be loved and cared for,
must be treated with highest respect.
the elders of the race
are the reason we are here.

HAKI MADHUBUTI

I'm **P**aula the cat
not thin nor fat
as happy as house cats can be

But now I've the urge
for my spirit to surge
and I shall go off
to sea

My hair, a hive of honey bees
Is a **Q**ueenly glory
Crackles like castanets
Hums like marimbas.

MAYA ANGELOU

Roll Jordan roll,
Roll Jordan roll,
I want to go to Heaven when I die
To hear old Jordan roll.

BLACK AMERICAN SPIRITUAL

To **S**atch

Sometimes I feel like I will *never* stop
Just go on forever
Till one fine mornin
I'm gonna reach up and grab me a handfulla stars
Swing out my long lean leg
And whip three hot strikes burnin down the heavens
And look over at God and say
How about that!

SAMUEL ALLEN

There is a heaven, for ever, day by day,
The upward longing of my soul doth tell me so.
There is a hell, I'm quite as sure; for pray,
If there were not, where would my neighbours go?

PAUL LAURENCE DUNBAR

Calling black people
Calling all black people, man woman child
Wherever you are, calling you, Urgent, come in
Black People, come in, wherever you are, urgent, calling
you, calling all black people
calling all black people, come in, black people, come
on in.

IMAMU AMIRI BARAKA

Your **V**ividness grants color where
Great need is, in this dingy town,
As you in pride of rose and brown
Thread the dull thoroughfare.

STERLING BROWN

W

Who
can be born black
and not
sing
the wonder of it
the joy
the
challenge

Who
can be born
black
and not exult!

MARI EVANS

X

Without e**X**pectation
there is no end
to the shock of morning
or even a small summer.

AUDRE LORDE

Young Neptune dashed the waters
Against enamel shore,
And kept the air a-tumbling
With bubble-clouds galore.

JAMES EMANUEL

Night's brittle song, sliver-thin,
Shatters into a billion fragments
Of quiet shadows
At the blaring jaZZ
Of a morning sun.

FRANK MARSHALL DAVIS

• ACKNOWLEDGMENTS •

The following acknowledgments of copyright permissions have been arranged in the order in which the material appears in this book. An asterisk (*) after the letter indicates that the selection is a complete poem, though perhaps taken from a longer work. A cross (†) after the letter indicates that the selection is a fragment of a longer work.

**Every effort has been made to trace the ownership of all copyrighted material and to secure permissions to reprint these selections. In the event of any question arising as to the use of any material, the editor and publisher, while expressing regret for any inadvertent error, will be happy to make the necessary correction in future printings. Thanks are due to the following for permission to reprint the selections below:

A †   from GOD'S TROMBONES by James Weldon Johnson, published by The Viking Press, 1927.

B †   from BLACK MAGIC by Dudley Randall—from the book LOVE YOU. Copyright © 1970 by Dudley Randall. Used by permission of the author.

C *   "Stars", copyright © 1975 by Robert Hayden, from ANGLE OF ASCENT: New and Selected Poems by Robert Hayden. Reprinted by permission of Liveright Publishing Corporation.

D *   "First Came L.E. Phants Letter" from THE LOST ZOO by Countee Cullen. Copyright © 1940 by Countee Cullen. Copyrights held by The Amistad Research Center, Tulane University, New Orleans, Louisiana. Administered by Thompson and Thompson, New York, N.Y.

E †   from "Greatness" which appeared in KNEES OF A NATURAL MAN, Selected Poetry of Henry Dumas, copyright © 1989 by Henry Dumas.**

F †   four lines from "Refugee in America". From SELECTED POEMS by Langston Hughes. Copyright 1943 by The Curtis Publishing Co. Reprinted by permission of Alfred A. Knopf, Inc.

G *   "God Never Planted a Garden". Permission granted by J. Lee Greene, from TIME'S UNFADING GARDEN: ANNE SPENCER'S LIFE AND POETRY (1977).

H †   "Harriet Tubman" from HONEY, I LOVE. Text copyright © 1978 by Eloise Greenfield.

I *   XVII from 26 WAYS OF LOOKING AT A BLACK MAN. Permission granted by Raymond R. Patterson, from 26 WAYS OF LOOKING AT A BLACK MAN: AND OTHER POEMS (1969).

J †   Excerpt from "Augustus Observes the Sunset", from Rita Dove, SELECTED POEMS, Pantheon/Vintage, copyright 1980, 1993 by Rita Dove. Used by permission of the author.

K †   from "I Am A Black"—CHILDREN COMING HOME, by Gwendolyn Brooks. Published by the David Company, Chicago, Illinois. Copyright © 1991. Used by permission of the author.

L *   LUCILLE CLIFTON: "the lesson of the falling leaves" copyright © 1987 by Lucille Clifton. Reprinted from GOOD WOMAN: POEMS AND A MEMOIR 1969–1980, by Lucille Clifton, with the permission of BOA Editions, Ltd., 92 Park Ave., Brockport, N.Y. 14420.

M †   from "Lineage" from FOR MY PEOPLE by Margaret Walker.**

N †   Excerpt from "Circle One" from POWERFUL LONG LADDER by Owen Dodson. Copyright © 1946 and copyright renewed © 1973 by Owen Dodson. Reprinted by permission of Farrar, Straus & Giroux, Inc.

O *   from BOOK OF LIFE by Haki Madhubuti, copyright © 1973.**

P †   "Paula the Cat" by Nikki Giovanni.**

Q *   from NOW SHEBA SINGS THE SONG by Maya Angelou, illustrated by Tom Feelings. Copyright © 1987 by Maya Angelou, text. Copyright © 1987 by Tom Feelings, illustrations. Used by permission of Dial Books for Young Readers, a division of Penguin Books USA, Inc.

R †   Black American Spiritual

S *   from IVORY TUSKS AND OTHER POEMS. Copyright © 1968 by Samuel W. Allen, used by permission of the author.

T *   "Theology" by Paul Laurence Dunbar from I GREET THE DAWN, poems by Paul Laurence Dunbar, selected by Ashley Bryan, Atheneum, New York, 1978.

U *   "SOS" from BLACK MAGIC POETRY 1961–1967 by Imamu Amiri Baraka. Reprinted by permission of Sterling Lord Literistic Inc. © 1965 by Amiri Baraka.

V †   four lines from "To Sally, Walking" from SOUTHERN ROAD by Sterling A. Brown. Copyright 1932 by Harcourt, Brace, & Co. Copyright renewed 1960 by Sterling Brown. Included in The COLLECTED POEMS OF STERLING A. BROWN, selected by Michael S. Harper. Copyright © 1980 by Sterling A. Brown. Reprinted by permission of HarperCollins Publishers, Inc.

W *   "Who Can Be Born Black" from I AM A BLACK WOMAN by Mari Evans.**

X †   from "Summer Oracle", copyright © 1992, 1973, 1970, 1968 by Audre Lorde, from UNDERSONG: Chosen Poems Old and New by Audre Lorde. Reprinted by permission of W. W. Norton & Company, Inc.

Y †   from "The Voyage of Jimmy Poo" from THE TREEHOUSE by James Emanuel.**

Z *   from "Four Glimpses of Night" by Frank Marshall Davis.**